OLIVER HAS A S...

BY

PIONEER VALLEY EDUCATIONAL PRESS, INC.

Look at Oliver.

Oliver is hungry.

"Meow!" said Oliver.

"Meow!"

Look!

Here are snacks.

"Meow!" said Oliver.

Look at the chips.

"Meow!" said Oliver.

Look at the cookies.

"Meow!" said Oliver.

Look at the pretzels.

"Meow!" said Oliver.

Look at the popcorn.

"Meow!" said Oliver.

Look at the mess.
"Meow!" said Oliver.
"Meow! Meow!"